OI FROG!

Kes Gray
and **Jim Field**

h
Hodder
Children's
Books

A division of Hachette Children's Books

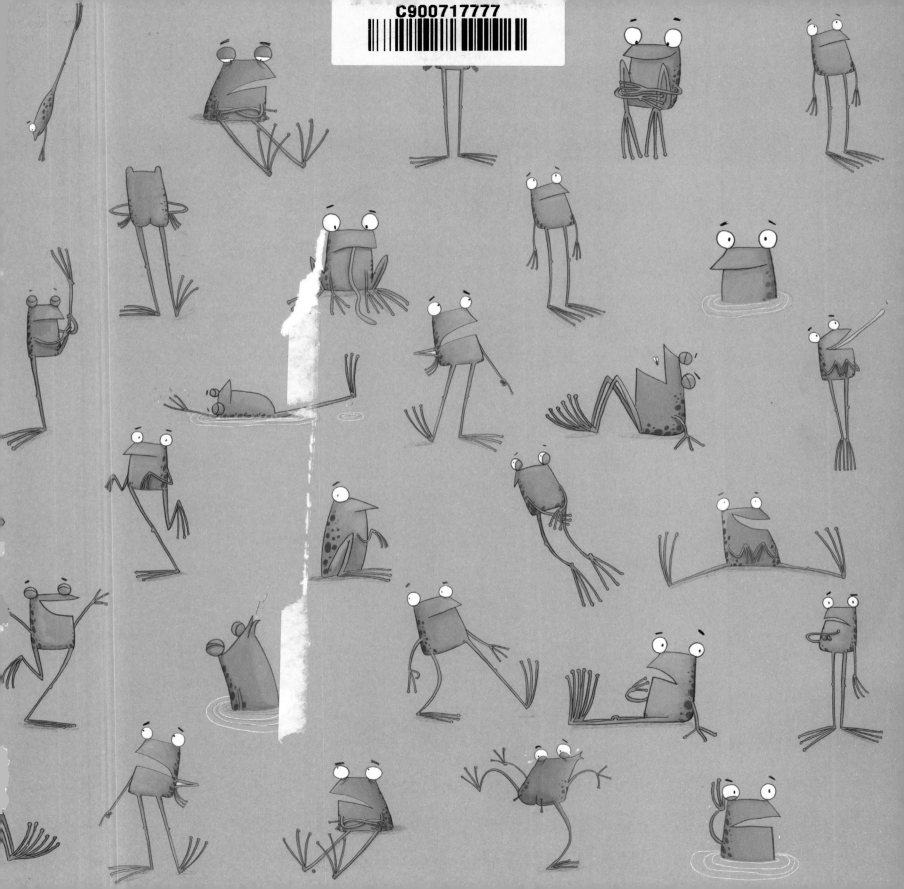

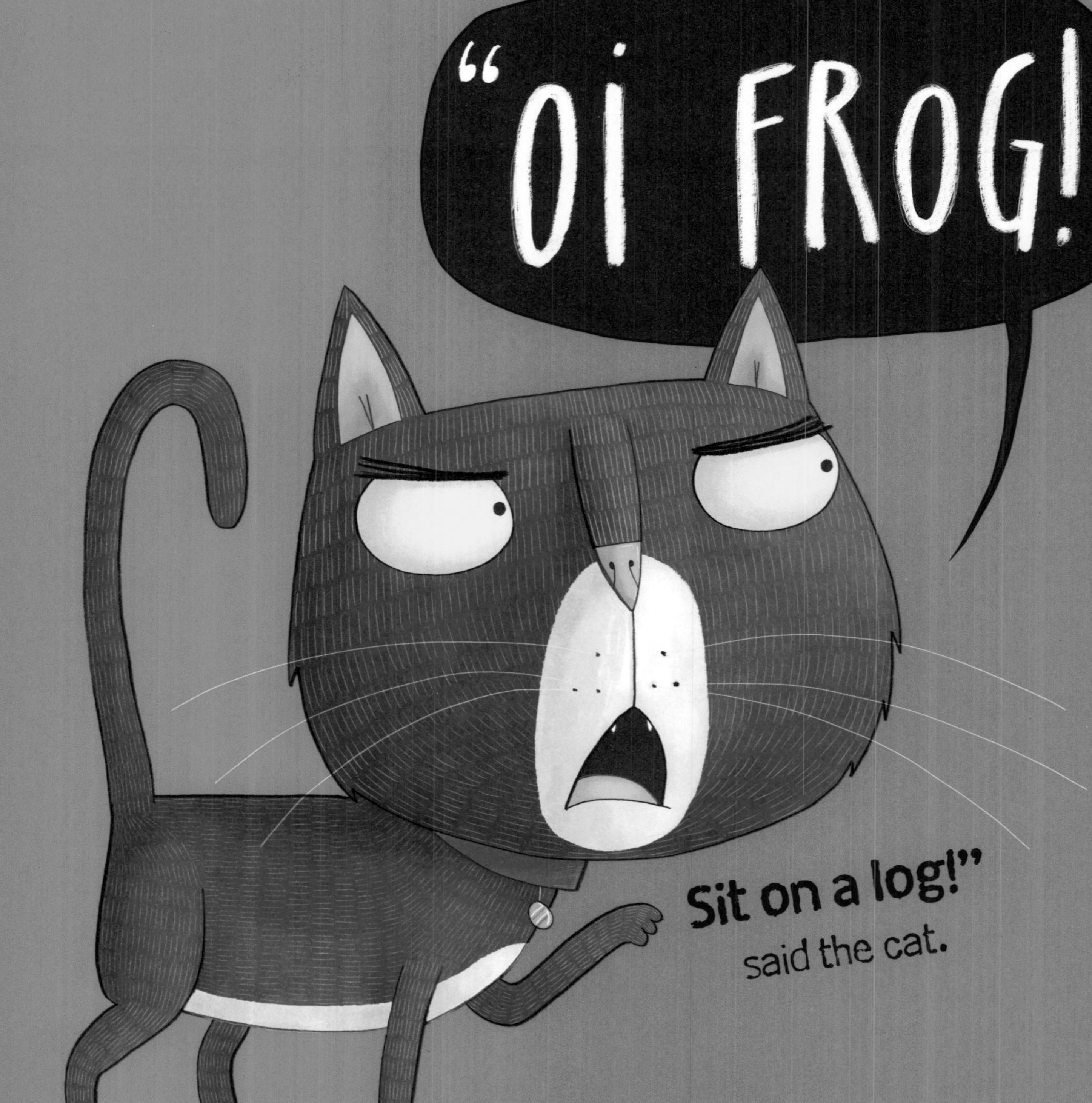

Sit on a log!"

said the cat.

To Linda, without whom a very small part of this book would not have been possible! K.G.

In loving memory of Joan and Ian J.F.

First published in 2014 by Hodder Children's Books

Text copyright © Kes Gray 2014
Illustration copyright © Jim Field 2014

Hodder Children's Books
338 Euston Road, London NW1 3BH

Hodder Children's Books Australia
Level 17/207 Kent Street, Sydney, NSW 2000

The right of Kes Gray to be identified as the author and Jim Field
as the illustrator of this Work has been asserted by them in accordance
with the Copyright, Designs and Patents Act 1988.

A catalogue record of this book is available from the British Library.

ISBN: 978 1 444 91085 8
10 9 8 7 6 5 4 3 2 1

Printed in China

Hodder Children's Books is a division of Hachette Children's Books.
An Hachette UK Company

www.hachette.co.uk

www.kesgray.com   www.jimfield.co.uk

"But I don't want to **sit** on a **log**," said the frog.
"Logs are all nobbly and uncomfortable.
And they can give you splinters in your bottom."

"I don't care," said the cat.
"You're a **frog**, so you must sit on a **log**."

"Can't I sit on a **mat?**" asked the frog.

"**Only** cats sit on **mats**," said the cat.

"What about a **chair?**"
said the frog.
"I wouldn't mind sitting
on a chair."

"**Hares** sit on **chairs,**"
said the cat.

"Perhaps I could I sit on a **stool?**" said the frog.

"**Mules** sit on **stools**,"
said the cat.

"What about a **sofa?**" said the frog.
"I could **stretch right out** on a sofa!"

"**Gophers** sit on **sofas,**" said the cat.

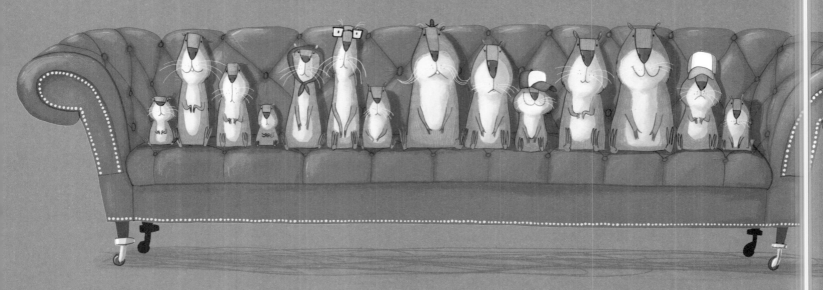

"It's very simple really.

"What do **lions** sit on?"
asked the frog.

"Lions sit on **irons,"**
said the cat.

"**Ouch!**" said the frog.
"What do **parrots** sit on?"

"**Parrots** sit on **carrots**,"
said the cat.

"**Lions**
sit on
irons
and
parrots
sit on
carrots."

"Doesn't sound very comfortable," said the frog.

"It's not about being comfortable," said the cat. "It's about doing the **right thing.**"

"What do **foxes** sit on?" asked the frog.

"**Foxes** sit on **boxes**," said the cat.

"**Foxes** sit on **boxes** and **fleas** sit on peas."

"What do **goats** sit on?" asked the frog.

"**Goats** sit on **coats**," said the cat.

"**Goats** sit on **coats**, **cows** sit on **ploughs** and **storks** sit on **forks**."

"What do **gorillas** sit on?"
asked the frog.

"**Gorillas**
sit on
pillars,"
said the cat.

"**Gorillas** sit on **pillars,**

rats sit on hats, weasels sit on easels and moles sit on poles."

"What do **seals** sit on?" asked the frog.

"Don't you know **anything?**"
said the cat.

"**Seals** sit on **wheels,**

doves sit on **gloves**,
newts sit on **flutes**,
lizards sit on **wizards** and
apes sit on **grapes**."

"What about **puffins?**" asked the frog.

"**Puffins** sit on **muffins**," said the cat.

"**Puffins** sit on **muffins**,

snakes sit on **cakes**,

owls sit on **towels**,

gibbons sit on **ribbons**,

lambs sit on **jams**,

and **bees** sit on **keys**."

"Well I **never** knew that," said the frog.

"Well you do now," said the cat.

"I was hoping you weren't going to ask that," said the cat...